Phoebe's Extraordinary Wings

Rachel Janel

DEDICATION

Autumn, Giorgi and Gabriella~ Everything I needed to know for this life I've learned because of the three of you. I'm so grateful for this journey and the beauty that continues to grow from it. Thank you for being my reason.

Dave, you've been my rock during this process. Thank you for all your patience, time, and energy in seeing this book through to completion.

Phoebe was an ordinary girl
With ordinary shoes and ordinary curls

Phoebe dreamed of a land
Of which she once heard
Where the ordinary kids played

In a not so ordinary world.
A world where kids once soared and flipped
And spun and twirled

Phoebe wanted to know
How she could be
Like all those magical kids
She wished she could see

She closed her eyes
And before her appeared

A kind, soft spoken man with white hair and a beard.
He leaned in and he promised to speak
Of a secret from a time long ago.
But before he began, he whispered a strange thing,
"Phoebe," he said, "You must promise to tell
Every ordinary kid that you know.
He said, "All around you, you see
Kids with no joy, kids who are not free.
What I'm about to tell you,
You must not keep to yourself, for it's too good to hide
Sadly, it was forgotten, and hidden by pride

"You see," he began, "the Not-So-Ordinary kids
Were special, they were magical
Because of the deliciously magical things they put inside
Those things, only the Earth can provide
Things that are real, things that are great."

"The ONLY things we had
From zero to one-hundred and eight
They were fresh
They were sweet
They brought life
From your head to your feet!"

"This isn't the magic you've heard of in tales
It cannot be made
With potion or spells
This magic I speak of
Is a gift from above
For all living things delivered with love."

"For these splendid bodies,
No food is greater
Than the food that is made
By our Majestic Creator."

"These glorious people of which we now speak
Were very different from you and from me
With their legs, how they would climb!
With their mouths, how they could sing!"

"Some believed they could even fly!"

Phoebes eyes grew very wide
As she imagined
Her own colorful ride

"From morning till night
They danced and they played
They were filled with the magic
They thought it would stay.
But one day,
A strange man came into town.
His name was Mr. Lyre N. Theefe
And he stole from the ground."

"He gave out tricks he falsely called food.
They were shiny and tasty
And for a moment seemed good."

Chocolate   Cookies   J

"But his biggest trick fooled us all.
Aisles and aisles were filled with his tricks
Would you believe the people begged for MORE though
His tricks made them sick!?!"

"You see, they became confused and quite dizzy,
They had headaches, bellyaches, fevers, and sores,
Allergies, nightmares, itches and more!!
They were in a terrible tizzy!!

"But sadly, it did not stop there
Mr. Lyre Theefe Man delighted in all he had done
And to be sure he fooled, well, everyone,
He began to add fake colors and flavors
Pretty wrappers and more
The whole town was now fooled
Of that you can be sure."

"As you can see,
They became quite lost.
They lost their smiles
They lost their power
They lost their sight
They scratched their skin by the hour!
Every last ounce of wisdom was gone
Sad, lonely and confused,
It was hard to go on.
Much to the surprise of these once magical beings,

Their magic had been traded
For terribly fake things
If only they had known
If only someone had told them
Not to trust thieves
Before their magic was stolen."

Phoebe felt sad
A little hopeless too
But with a spark in her wings,
She shouted,
"There must be a way,
What can I do?!"
She began to feel hope
Her magic wasn't gone
Willing and ready,
She shouted, "They HAVE to go on!
There MUST be a way!
Please tell me how,
How can I help?!
I need to know NOW!"
"You must TELL them Phoebe,
And show them too.
They need to see
The magic in YOU.
All is not lost.
They can learn the old way.
They can regain their magic.
It can be here to stay."

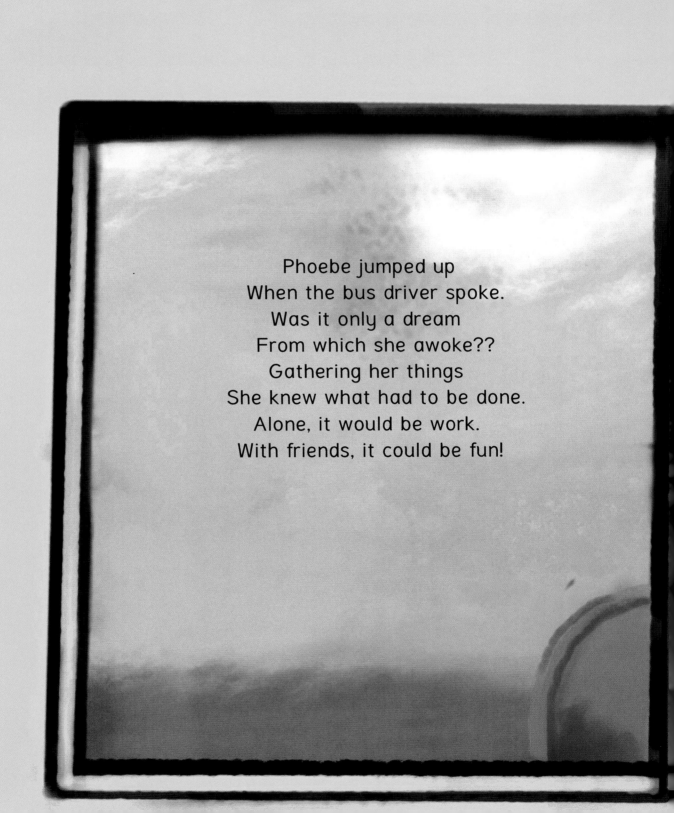

Phoebe jumped up
When the bus driver spoke.
Was it only a dream
From which she awoke??
Gathering her things
She knew what had to be done.
Alone, it would be work.
With friends, it could be fun!

She went into school
As fast as she could
She had an idea
She knew would be good.
About to have breakfast
Were friends she knew well,
Aidan and Maddie
And Lucas and Jake
Getting ready to eat
Cookies, candies, soda, and cake.
Sugary junk that was terribly fake!
"Nooooo! Don't eat that!" She shouted.
There are better things to eat!
Apples, mangos, oranges and beets
Are only SOME
Of the amazing magical treats!
Try it, taste it, see with your eyes!
They're naturally sweet!
They're the best kind of prize!
They look good, they taste good,
They feel good to eat.
They take away your sickies,
Your belly aches and even stinky feet!
Throw away those fake sugary treats!
Because treats are not treats
If they make you sick
From your head to your feet!

She caught the attention
Of all who were near
They gathered around
They wanted to hear
She invited kids, teachers,
The principle too,
Excited to share
The plans that she drew!
She said, "If you plant and grow
The foods that you eat
You'll be filled with the magic
From your head to your feet!"
Looking at Phoebe
They could see it was true
They knew now,
All they must do!

They looked in their cabinets
They looked in their drawers
They threw out the junk
As they shouted, "NO MORE!"

The people shared
Seeds, shovels, and rakes
Planting glorious gardens,
They spent most of their days.
When nighttime came
They gathered around
They shared in the joy
With the friends they had found.

Day after day
They looked and felt better.
They enjoyed new foods
Whole fruits, veggies and cheddar
They thanked Phoebe for sharing
The magic she found
The magic in food
That comes from the ground.

Is this a true tale?
Would you like to know?
Plant a seed.
Help it grow.
Grow your own magic
In a garden of fun.
Share with your neighbor
Real food is for everyone!

Made in the USA
Columbia, SC
18 December 2020